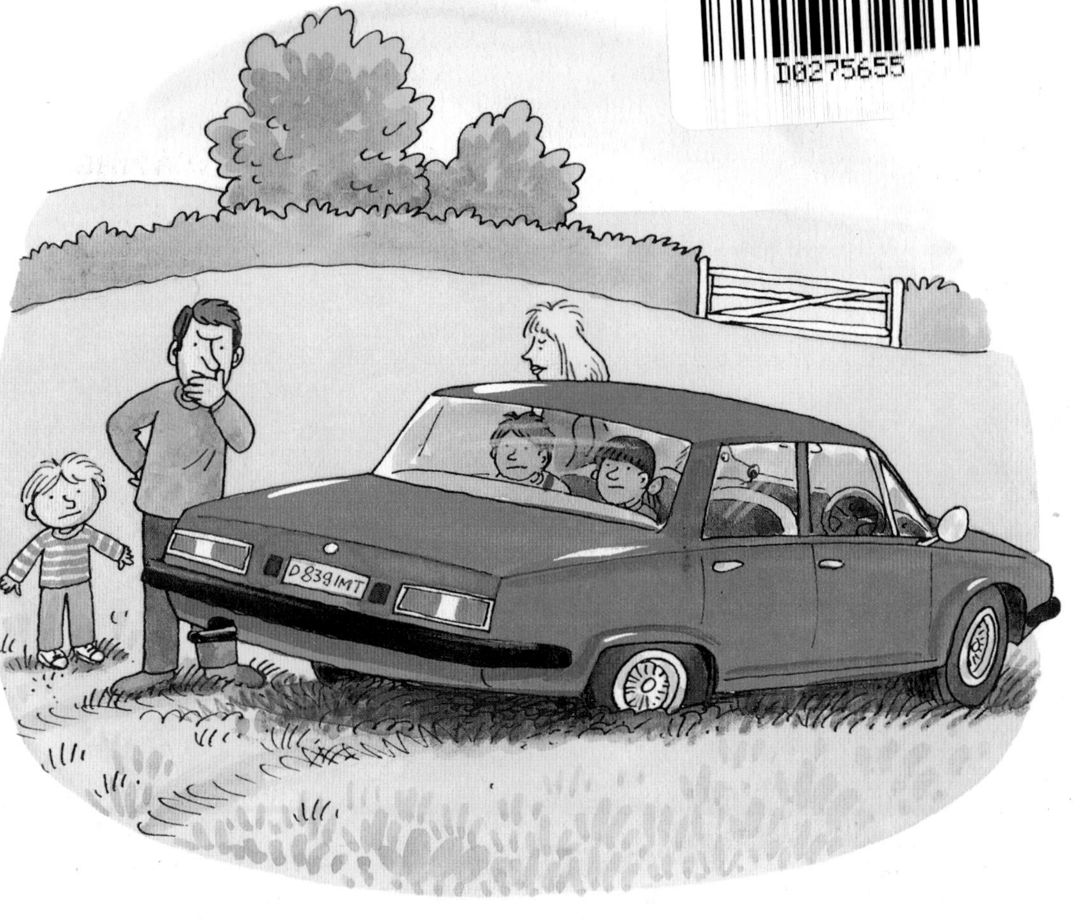

The car was stuck.

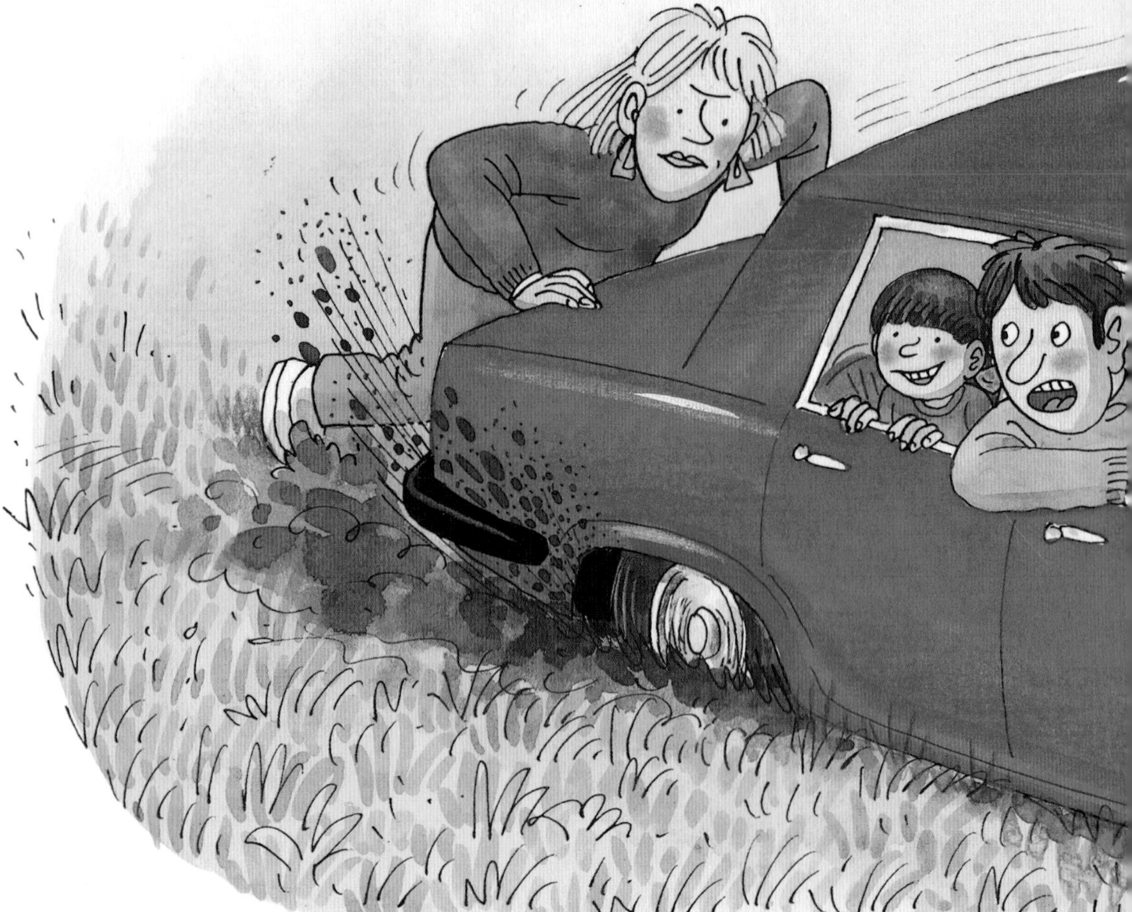

Mum pushed it.

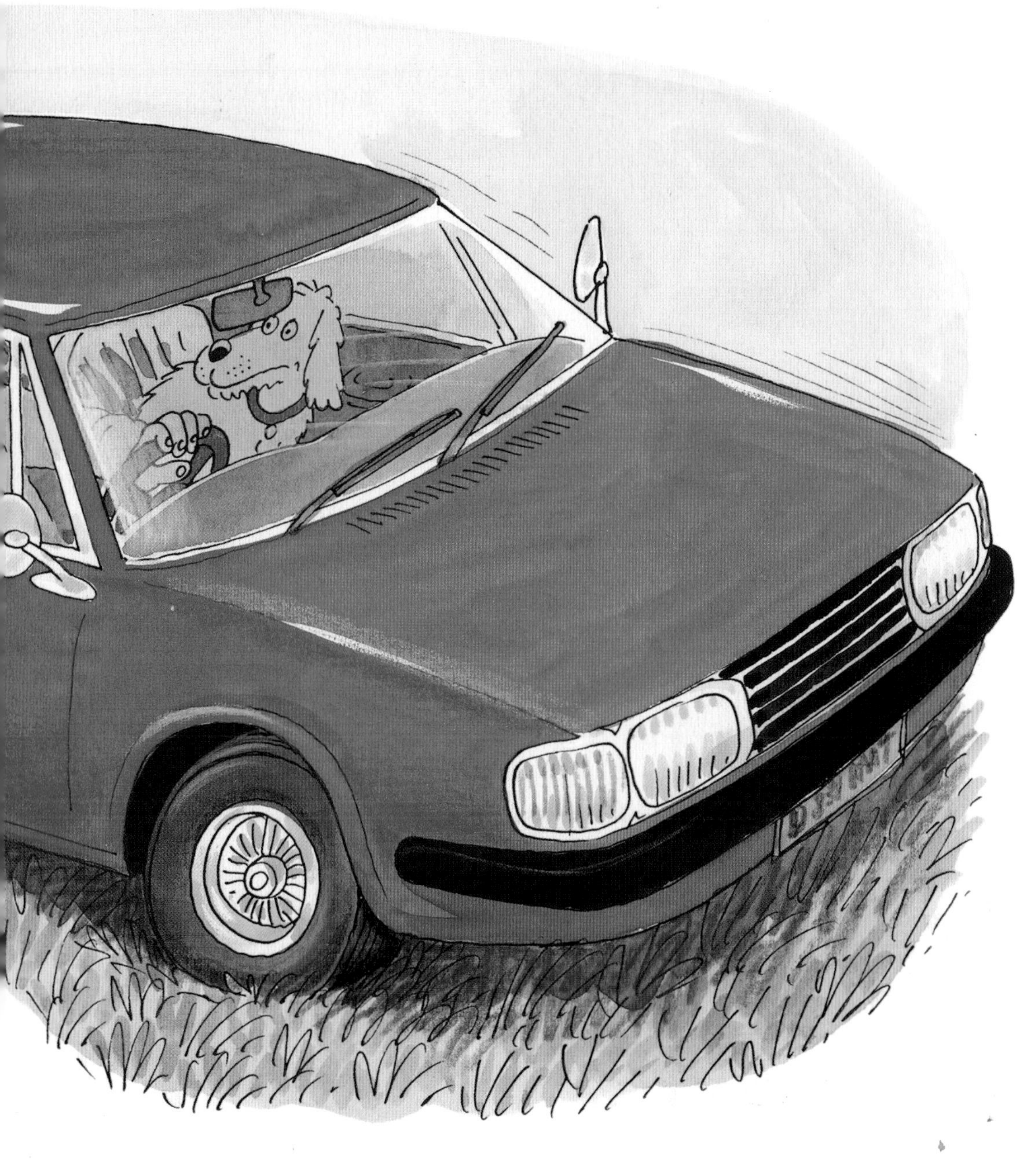

Biff and Chip pushed it.

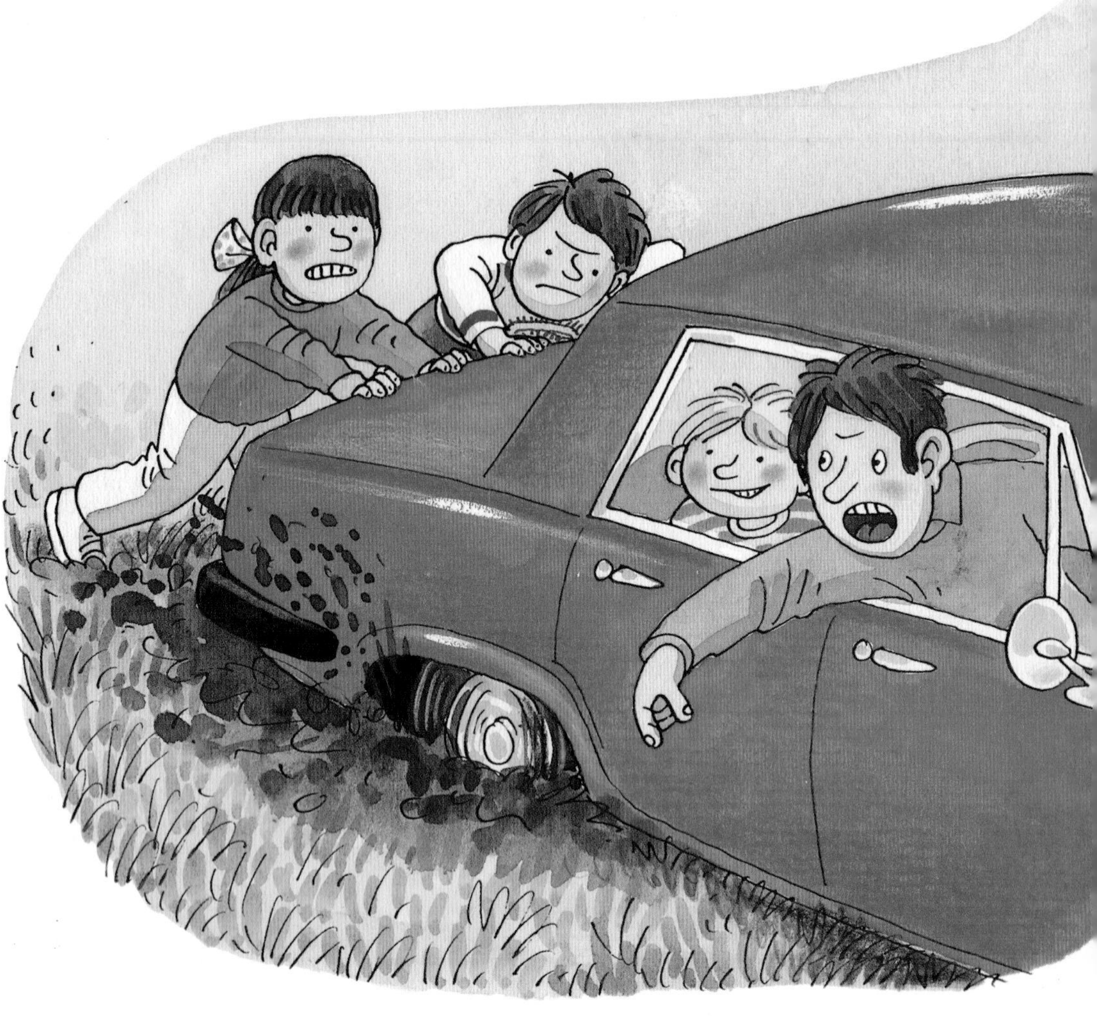

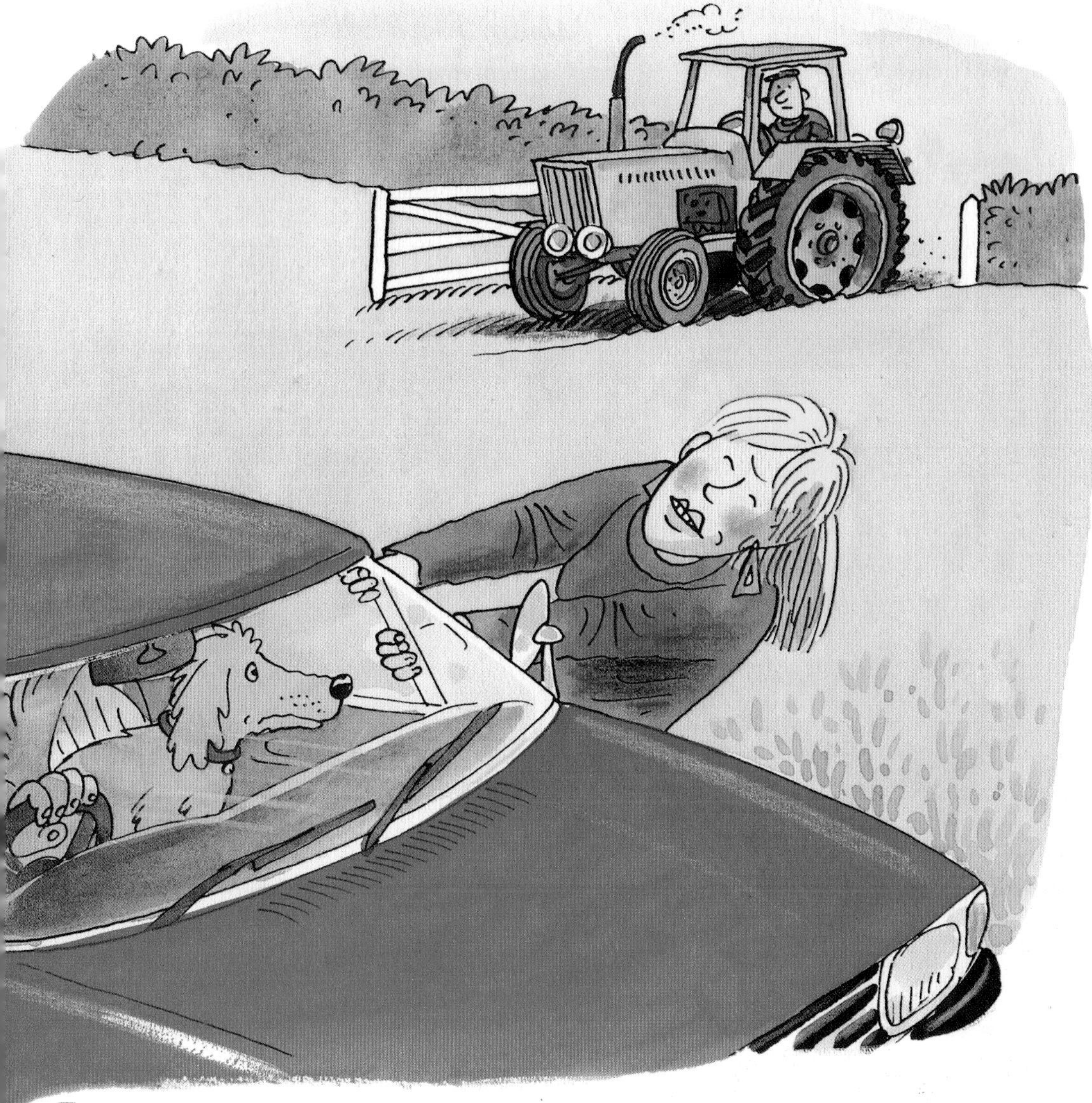

Mum pulled it.

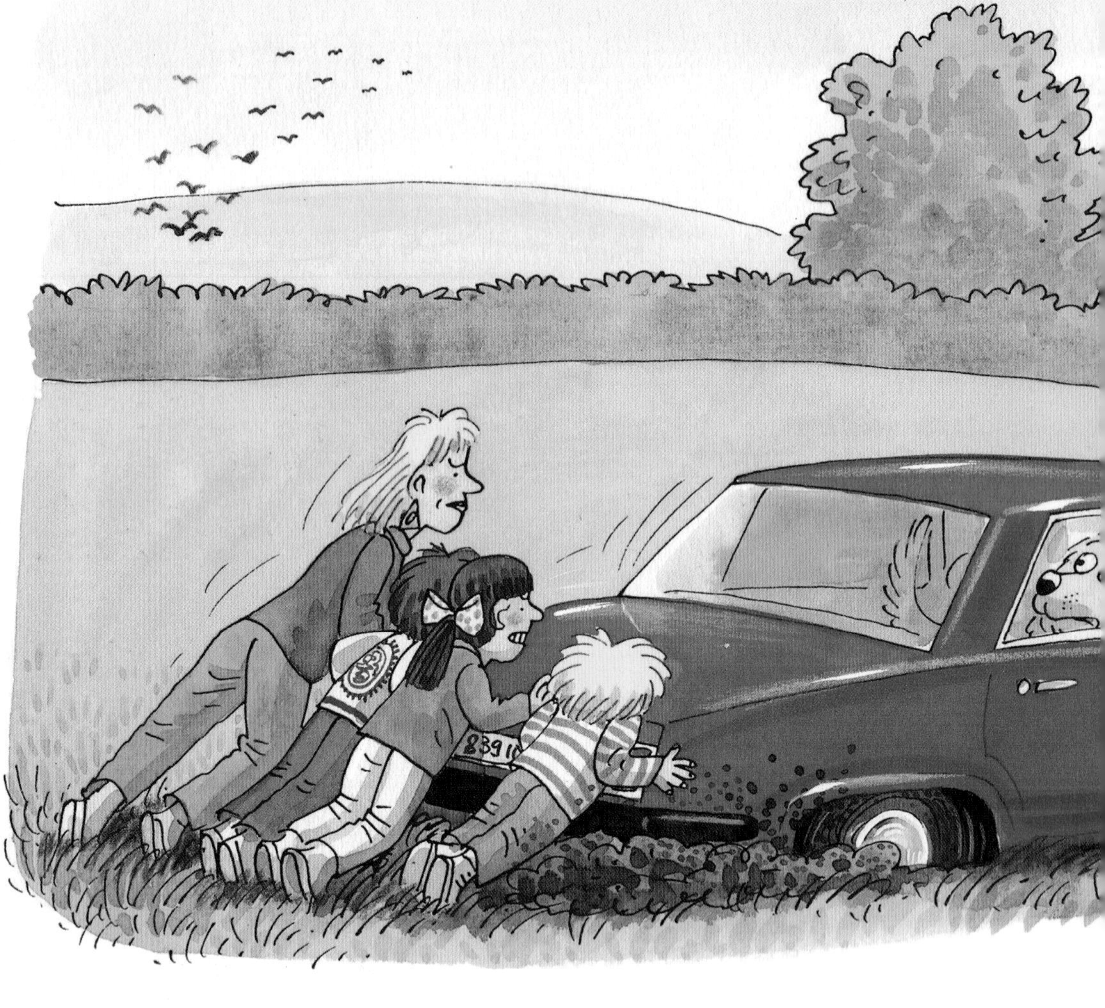

The tractor pulled it.

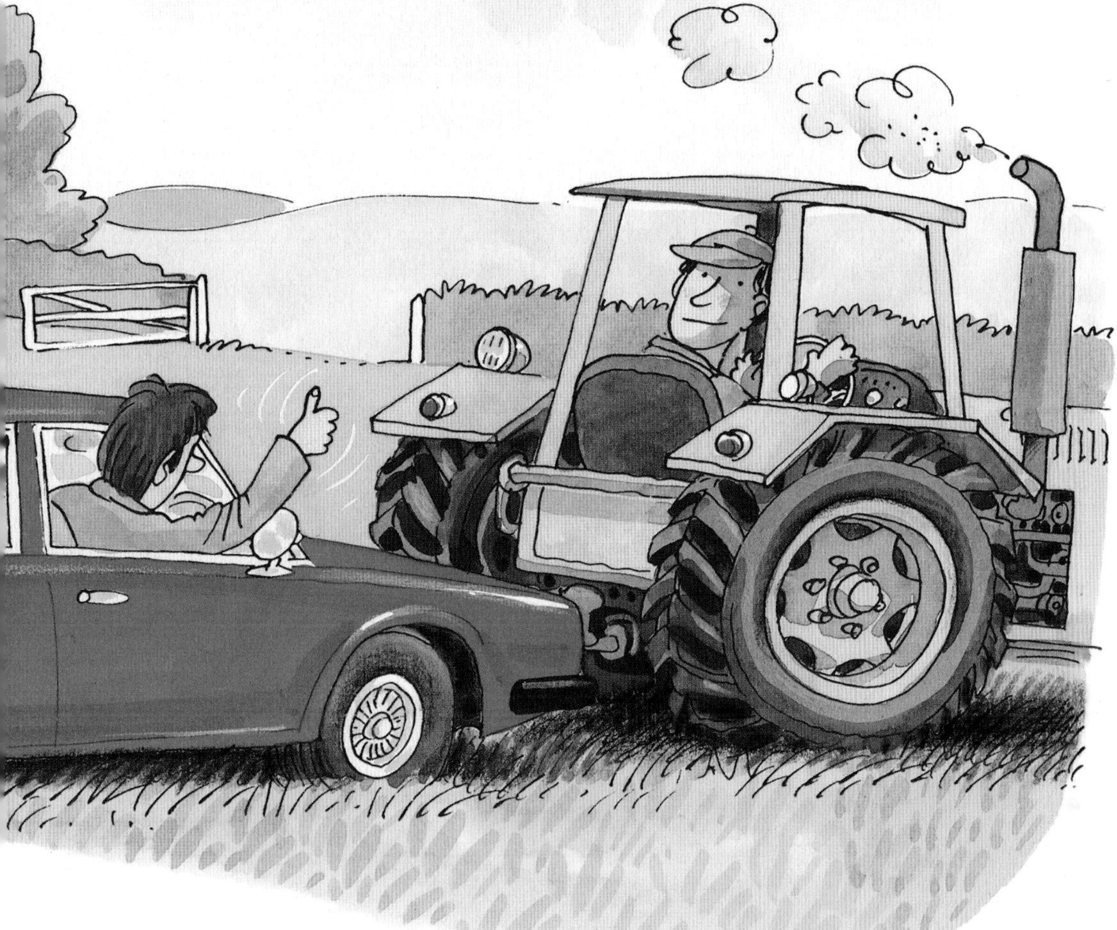

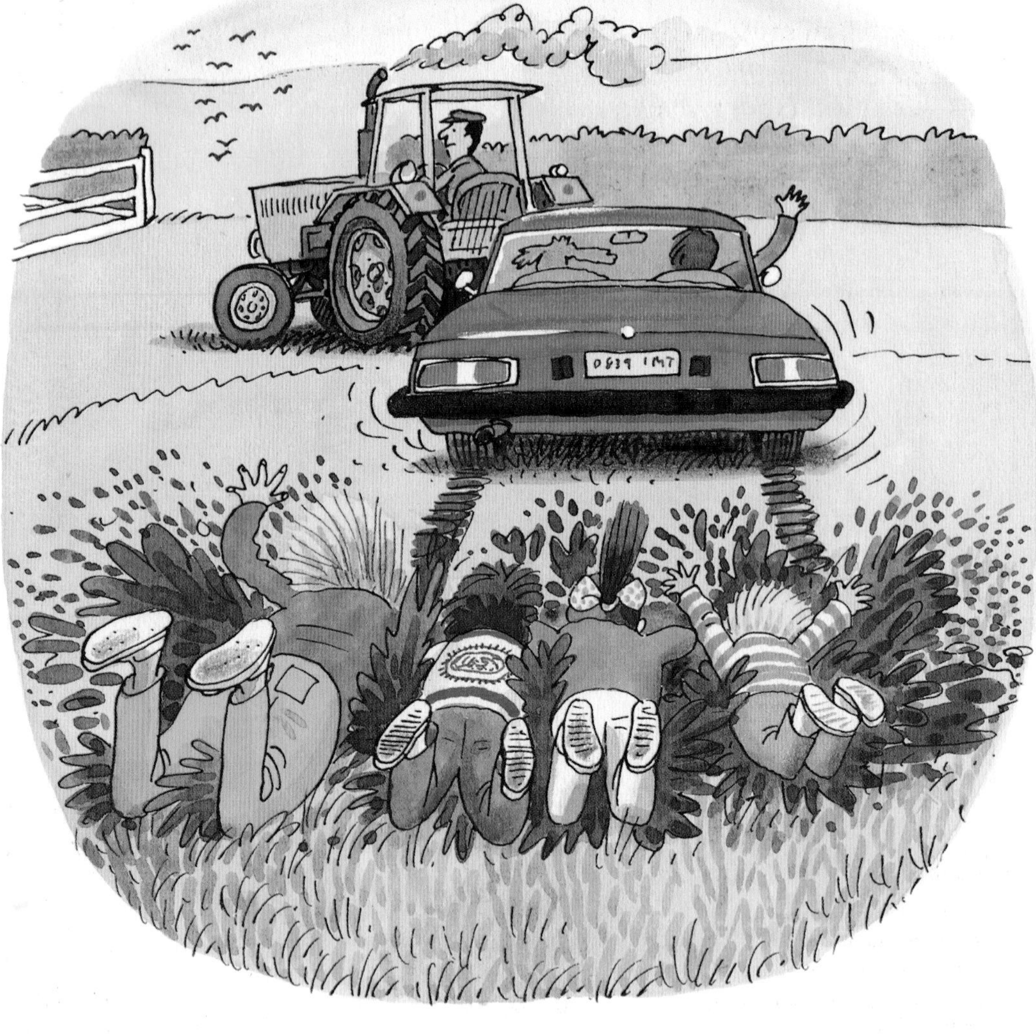

Oh no!